THE ONCE LONELY GHOST

The Once Lonely Ghost

VICKI LOMBARDI

Nadia Popova

To my children,

Your love of books is inspiring. Thank you for asking me to make up stories to tell you.

To my husband,

Thank you for motivating me to write and publish a children's book. Without your support and encouragement, this would not have been possible.

Text Copyright © 2021
Written by Vicki Lombardi
Illustrated by Nadia Popova
Edited by Aimee Roberts

First Printing, 2022

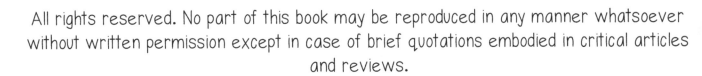

sits a weathered, old house
at the edge of Town Square.

As night falls an
the townspeopl
get sleepy
"BOO BOO" i
what they hear
which sounds
little creepy

"No one lives there. It's been vacant 50 years!" says the small town's mayor, Mrs. Mary McLeers.

But if you look past
the chipped paint,
rubble, and rot,
you'll see what's
inside is not at all
what they thought.

It's not scary
or spooky.
The house
has a host.
Inside lives
a tiny, friendly
ghost!

No family or friends. The ghost lives on his own. He is sad, you see, because he's always alone.

He cries out, "BOO HOO", and from his face falls a tear. While a haunted sound is what the outsiders hear.

Little Ghost is hopeful. It is soon
Halloween! He can leave his house
without being "seen".

Everyone dresses up for fun trick-or-treating.

Maybe they'll think he's in costume when he finally makes a greeting!

When it's time for children to walk door-to-door, the little ghost leaves home and begins to explore!

He smiles at all of the happy people
passing by, and when he feels bravest
of all, shouts a great big "HI!"

When the townspeople hear him, they also say "Hi." Relieved, the little lonely ghost smiles and sighs.

Despite his appearance, they learn
he's quite nice!

He's just lonely, but
friendly, to be precise!

The brave little ghost conquered his fear and can now welcome visitors every month of the year!

Once the townspeople looked past
the house and saw
who lived within,

the once lonely ghost let
his new life begin!

Printed in the USA
CPSIA information can be obtained
at www.ICGtesting.com